D0553603

G. Washington

GEORGE WASHINGTON
(1732-1799)

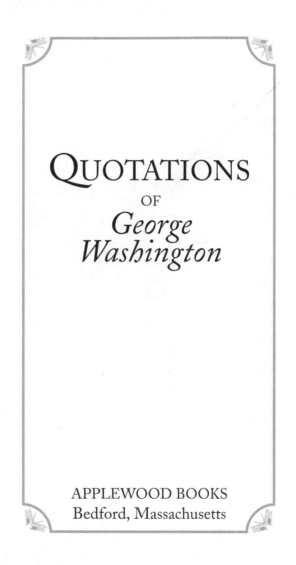

QUOTATIONS
OF
George Washington

APPLEWOOD BOOKS
Bedford, Massachusetts

Copyright ©2003 Applewood Books, Inc.

Thank you for purchasing an Applewood Book.
Applewood reprints America's lively classics—
books from the past that are still of interest to
modern readers. For a free copy of our current
catalog, please write to Applewood Books,
P.O. Box 365, Bedford, MA 01730.

ISBN 978-1-55709-937-2

10 9 8 7 6

Manufactured in U.S.A.

George Washington

GEORGE WASHINGTON was born in Virginia in 1732. As a young man, he learned the morals, manners, and knowledge necessary to become a Virginia gentleman.

He was particularly interested in the military arts and western expansion. At the age of sixteen, he helped survey Shenandoah lands. At the age of twenty-two, he was commissioned a lieutenant colonel and fought in the first battles of what became the French and Indian War.

After his military service and before the American Revolution, Washington served in the Virginia House of Burgesses and managed his lands around Mount Vernon. As with other planters, Washington felt exploited by increasing British restrictions. As these feelings accelerated, Washington found himself speaking out.

In 1775, Washington attended the Second Continental Congress in Philadelphia where he was elected Commander in Chief of the Continental Army. On July 3, 1775, at Cambridge, Massachusetts, he took command of his ragged troops. After six years, through the elements of surprise and perseverance, Washington and his troops were victorious.

After Cornwallis surrendered in 1781, Washington wanted to return to Mount Vernon. But the new nation required leadership, and Washington was thrust into service. When the Constitution was ratified, the Electoral College unanimously elected him our President.

He served two terms and then, feeling old and weary of politics, retired back to the fields of Mount Vernon. There, he spent less than three years before he passed away on December 14, 1799.

QUOTATIONS
OF
George Washington

*I*t is better to offer no excuse than a bad one.

G. Washington

*A*ll I am I owe to my mother. I attribute all my success in life to the moral, intellectual and physical education I received from her.

G. Washington

*N*o man, who is profligate in his morals, or a bad member of the civil community, can possibly be a true Christian, or a credit to his own religious society.

G. Washington

*T*o be prepared for war is one of the most effectual means of preserving peace.

*D*iscipline is the soul of an army. It makes small numbers formidable; procures success to the weak, and esteem to all.

G Washington

*W*hen a people shall have become incapable of governing themselves and fit for a master, it is of little consequence from what quarter he comes.

G Washington

I am persuaded, you will permit me to observe that the path of true piety is so plain as to require but little political direction. To this consideration we ought to ascribe the absence of any regulation, respecting religion, from the Magna-Charta of our country.

G Washington

A free people ought not only to be armed, but disciplined.

We ought not to look back unless it is to derive useful lessons from past errors, and for the purpose of profiting by dear-bought experience.

G. Washington

Government being, among other pur-poses, instituted to protect the persons and consciences of men from oppression, it cer-tainly is the duty of rulers, not only to abstain from it themselves, but, according to their stations, to prevent it in others.

G. Washington

I was summoned by my country, whose voice I can never hear but with veneration and love.

G. Washington

There is no restraining men's tongues or pens when charged with a little vanity.

 T he power under the constitution will always be in the people. It is entrusted for certain defined purposes, and for a certain limited period, to representatives of their own choosing; and whenever it is executed contrary to their interest, or not agreeable to their wishes, their servants can, and undoubtedly will be, recalled.

 W hen we assumed the soldier, we did not lay aside the citizen.

 B e courteous to all, but intimate with few, and let those few be well tried before you give them your confidence. True friendship is a plant of slow growth, and must undergo and withstand the shocks of adversity before it is entitled to the appellation.

 H appiness and moral duty are inseparably connected.

A slender acquaintance with the world must convince every man that actions, not words, are the true criterion of the attachment of friends; and that the most liberal professions of goodwill are very far from being the surest marks of it.

Washington

*I*f we cannot learn wisdom from experience, it is hard to say where it is to be found.

Washington

*M*ankind, when left to themselves, are unfit for their own government.

Washington

*T*he hand of providence has been so conspicuous in all this, that he must be worse than an infidel that lacks faith, and more than wicked, that has not gratitude enough to acknowledge his obligations.

*L*iberty, when it begins to take root, is a plant of rapid growth.

G. Washington

*T*he name of American, which belongs to you in your national capacity, must always exalt the just pride of patriotism more than any appellation derived from local discriminations.

G. Washington

*A*rbitrary power is most easily established on the ruins of liberty abused to licentiousness.

G. Washington

*N*othing is more harmful to the service, than the neglect of discipline for that discipline, more than numbers, gives one army superiority over another.

It is our duty to make the best of our misfortunes, and not to suffer passion to interfere with our interest and public good.

All possess alike liberty of conscience and immunities of citizenship.

Of all the dispositions and habits which lead to political prosperity, religion and morality are indispensable support. In vain would that man claim the tribute of patriotism who should labor to subvert these great pillars.

The basis of our political systems is the right of the people to make and to alter their constitutions of government. But the constitution which at any time exists, till changed by an explicit and authentic act of the whole people, is sacredly obligatory upon all.

I am sure that never was a people, who had more reason to acknowledge a Divine interposition in their affairs, then those of the United States; and I should be pained to believe that they have forgotten that agency, which was so often manifested during our Revolution, or that they failed to consider the omnipotence of that God who is alone able to protect them.

H armony, liberal intercourse with all nations, are recommended by policy, humanity, and interest.

A ssociate yourself with men of good quality if you esteem your own reputation; for 'tis better to be alone than in bad company.

T o err is nature, to rectify error is glory.

*A*s Mankind becomes more liberal, they will be more apt to allow that all those who conduct themselves as worthy members of the community are equally entitled to the protections of civil government. I hope ever to see America among the foremost nations of justice and liberality.

G. Washington

*T*o encourage literature and the arts is a duty which every good citizen owes to his country.

G. Washington

*F*ew men have virtue to withstand the highest bidder.

G. Washington

*I*t will be found an unjust and unwise jealousy to deprive a man of his natural liberty upon the supposition he may abuse it.

*T*o the efficacy and permanency of your Union, a government for the whole is indispensable. No alliance, however strict, between the parts can be an adequate substitute.

G. Washington

*I*t is well, I die hard, but I am not afraid to go.

G. Washington

*O*bserve good faith and justice toward all nations. Cultivate peace and harmony with all.

G. Washington

*H*ow far you go in life depends on your being tender with the young, compassionate with the aged, sympathetic with the striving, and tolerant of the weak and the strong. Because someday in life you will have been all of these.

*L*et us raise a standard to which the wise and honest can repair; the rest is in the hands of God.

G. Washington

*A*void the necessity of those overgrown military establishments, which, under any form of government, are inauspicious to liberty, and which are to be regarded as particularly hostile to Republican Liberty.

G. Washington

*T*he time is near at hand which must determine whether Americans are to be free men or slaves.

G. Washington

I had always hoped that this land might become a safe and agreeable asylum to the virtuous and persecuted part of mankind, to whatever nation they might belong.

*L*et your heart feel for the afflictions and distress of everyone, and let your hand give in proportion to your purse.

G. Washington

I do not mean to exclude altogether the idea of patriotism. I know it exists, and I know it has done much in the present contest. But I will venture to assert, that a great and lasting war can never be supported on this principle alone. It must be aided by a prospect of interest, or some reward.

G. Washington

*N*o people can be bound to acknowledge and adore the invisible hand which conducts the affairs of men more than the people of the United States.

G. Washington

*I*t is our true policy to steer clear of permanent alliances with any portion of the foreign world.

We must never despair; our situation has been compromising before, and it changed for the better; so I trust it will again. If difficulties arise, we must put forth new exertion and proportion our efforts to the exigencies of the times.

There can be no greater error than to expect, or calculate, upon real favors from nation to nation. It is an illusion which experience must cure, which a just pride ought to discard.

I know of no pursuit in which more real and important services can be rendered to any country than by improving its agriculture, its breed of useful animals, and other branches of a husbandman's cares.

There is nothing which can better deserve your patronage than the promotion of science and literature. Knowledge is in every country the surest basis of public happiness.

While men perform their social duties faithfully, they do all that society or the state can with propriety demand or expect; and remain responsible only to their Maker for their religion, or modes of faith, which they may prefer or profess.

The marvel of all history is the patience with which men and women submit to burdens unnecessarily laid upon them by their governments.

I walk on untrodden ground. There is scarcely any part of my conduct which may not hereafter be drawn into precedent.

G Washington

I n contemplating the causes which may disturb our Union, it occurs as matter of serious concern that any ground should have been furnished for characterizing parties by geographical discriminations, Northern and Southern, Atlantic and Western; whence designing men may endeavor to excite a belief that there is a real difference of local interests and views. One of the expedients of party to acquire influence within particular districts is to misrepresent the opinions and aims of other districts. You cannot shield yourselves too much against the jealousies and heart burnings which spring from these misrepresentations; they tend to render alien to each other those who ought to be bound together by fraternal affection.

T he Citizens of the United States of America have a right to applaud themselves for having given to mankind examples of an enlarged and liberal policy a policy worthy of imitation.

G Washington

I hope I shall always possess firmness and virtue enough to maintain what I consider the most enviable of all titles, the character of an honest man.

G Washington

M y manner of living is plain and I do not mean to be put out of it. A glass of wine and a bit of mutton are always ready and such as will be content to partake of them are always welcome. Those who expect more will be disappointed.

*I*f I could conceive that the general government might ever be so administered as to render the liberty of conscience insecure, I beg you will be persuaded, that no one would be more zealous than myself to establish effectual barriers against the horrors of spiritual tyranny, and every species of religious persecution.

G. Washington

*T*he liberty enjoyed by the people of these states of worshiping Almighty God agreeably to their consciences, is not only among the choicest of their blessings, but also of their rights.

G. Washington

*L*iberty itself will find in such a government, with powers properly distributed and adjusted, its surest guardian.

*L*enience will operate with greater force, in some instances than rigor. It is therefore my first wish to have all of my conduct distinguished by it.

G. Washington

*I*f in the opinion of the people the distribution or modification of the constitutional powers be in any particular wrong, let it be corrected by an amendment in the way which the Constitution designates, but let there be no change by usurpation; for though this in one instance may be the instrument of good, it is the customary weapon by which free governments are destroyed.

G. Washington

*L*et us with caution indulge the supposition that morality can be maintained without religion. Reason and experience both forbid us to expect that national morality can prevail in exclusion of religious principle.

*M*y observation is that whenever one person is found adequate to the discharge of a duty . . . it is worse executed by two persons, and scarcely done at all if three or more are employed therein.

G.Washington

*T*he fate of unborn millions will now depend, under God, on the courage of this army. Our cruel and unrelenting enemy leaves us only the choice of brave resistance, or the most abject submission. We have therefore, to resolve to conquer or die.

G.Washington

*I*n looking forward to the moment which is intended to terminate the career of my public life, my feelings do not permit me to suspend the deep acknowledgment of that debt of gratitude which I owe to my beloved country for the many honors it has conferred upon me.

*T*he very atmosphere of firearms any-
where and everywhere restrains evil inter-
ference—they deserve a place of honor
with all that is good.

G. Washington

*I*t is impossible to rightly govern the world
without God and the Bible.

G. Washington

*T*he preservation of the sacred fire of liberty, and the destiny of the Republican
model of Government, are justly consid-
ered as deeply, perhaps as finally staked, on
the experiment entrusted to the hands of
the American people.

G. Washington

*I*f we desire to avoid insult, we must be
able to repel it; if we desire to secure peace,
one of the most powerful instruments of
our rising prosperity, it must be known,
that we are at all times ready for war.

*T*he propitious smiles of Heaven can never be expected on a nation that disregards the eternal rules of order and right which Heaven itself has ordained.

*I*t may be laid down as a primary position, and the basis of our system, that every citizen who enjoys the protection of a free government, owes not only a proportion of his property, but even of his personal services to the defense of it.

*T*he magnitude and difficulty of the trust to which the voice of my country called me, being sufficient to awaken in the wisest and most experienced of her citizens a distrustful scrutiny into his qualifications, could not but overwhelm with despondence one who ought to be peculiarly conscious of his own deficiencies.

*E*very man, conducting himself as a good citizen, and being accountable to God alone for his religious opinions, ought to be protected in worshiping the Deity according to the dictates of his own conscience.

G.Washington.

*T*his government, the offspring of our own choice, uninfluenced and unawed, adopted upon full investigation and mature deliberation, completely free in its principles, in the distribution of its powers, uniting security with energy, and containing within itself a provision for its own amendment, has a just claim to your confidence and your support.

G.Washington.

*I*f I was to give indulgence to my inclinations, every moment that I could withdraw from the fatigues of my station should be spent in retirement.

Government is not reason; it is not eloquence; it is force! Like fire, it is a dangerous servant and a fearful master.

G Washington

However pacific the general policy of a Nation may be, it ought never to be without an adequate stock of Military knowledge for emergencies.

G Washington

The very idea of the power and the right of the People to establish Government presupposes the duty of every Individual to obey the established Government.

G Washington

The Great rule of conduct for us, in regard to foreign Nations is in extending our commercial relations to have with them as little political connection as possible.

Whatever may be conceded to the influence of refined education on minds of peculiar structure, reason and experience both forbid us to expect that National morality can prevail in exclusion of religious principle.

~ George Washington ~

It is a wonder to me, there should be found a single monarch, who does not realize that his own glory and felicity must depend on the prosperity and happiness of his People.

~ George Washington ~

I can truly say I had rather be at Mount Vernon with a friend or two about me, than to be attended at the Seat of Government by the Officers of State and the Representatives of every Power in Europe.

Knowledge is in every country the surest basis of public happiness. In one in which the measures of Government receive their impression so immediately from the sense of the Community as in ours it is proportionably essential.

G.Washington

Observe good faith and justice towards all Nations. Cultivate peace and harmony with all. Religion and morality enjoin this conduct; and can it be that good policy does not equally enjoin it? It will be worthy of a free, enlightened, and, at no distant period, a great Nation, to give to mankind the magnanimous and too novel example of a People always guided by an exalted justice and benevolence.

G.Washington

My first wish is to see this plague of mankind, war, banished from the earth.

*I*f after all my humble but faithful endeavours to advance the felicity of my Country and mankind, I may indulge a hope that my labours have not been altogether without success, it will be the only real compensation I can receive in the closing of life.

GWashington

*I*t is really a strange thing that there should not be room enough in the world for men to live, without cutting one anothers' throats.

GWashington

*U*nder a good government (which I have no doubt we shall establish) this Country certainly promises greater advantages, than almost any other, to persons of moderate property, who are determined to be sober, industrious and virtuous members of Society.

G. Washington